Satisfied

A Tale of Red Desire

By

Marcia Nicole

ISBN:
978-1-963764-78-9 (e-Book)
978-1-963764-79-6 (Paperback)

I – Awakening

"Oh, God!" She screamed. "Oh, fuck!"

Mercy couldn't help but curl up her toes as he sucked up the steadily flowing juices from her aching nub, each lick of his tongue eliciting a cry of intense sensations from her.

He switched things up every time she moaned. Between her thighs, his head remained in its position, one hand exploring the curves of her legs as the other roamed around her breasts, grabbing and touching at will.

She put a hand on his hair, pushing his head between her legs as her own hand looked for his other one, and she locked herself and him in a sexual embrace as he continued to work his magic on her pussy.

Mercy couldn't really tell where she was, only that *he* was there, and that *he* was going to rock her world.

On the bed, she could even feel his heat from a distance, his hard, aching member begging for release, to be able to find itself where it belonged and do the deed it was meant to do.

But this was too good to rush, and his tongue felt too perfectly shaped for her moistened nub as he expertly took her to the heights of orgasm, only to stop just at the edge and let her come back down again.

With labored breathing, she begged each time she was about to cum, but he wouldn't let her. No.

Right now, he had all the power, and she was putty in his hands; at his mercy.

He looked at her, or rather, at her love button, the place he was worshipping seconds before.

It was beautiful.

Like velvet curtains opening them up in invitation, guiding their guest of honor through the tunnel of love. Pink and red, with a little button jutting out of there.

Her clit.

And he knew just where to hit it where it…hurts? Maybe. Maybe it would. And it would hurt *so good*.

She screamed as he stimulated it with his hands, pulling it with his lips as it stretched from her pussy.

"Oh, Hiro, oh, *fuuuuuck*!" She screamed, the sensation was too much, too perfect, and too pleasurably painful for her not to be able to open up like she did.

She was like a fountain, a broken faucet, a dam finally opened, as her juices flowed like a shower upon him.

He closed his eyes and laughed, mouth open and teeth bared, ready to receive the gift of greatness from her.

"Fucccck! Aaaaaaa, fuuuuck!" She screamed, her pussy aching, her legs shaking, and hips following suit as she uncontrollably writhed on the bed, feeling the wetness of the sheets against her skin, the smell of sex pungent in the air after her explosive orgasm.

"Satisfied?" Hiro asked, his face a display of sheer pride as he looked upon her, licked his lips and around them as she looked at him back.

"Fuck yes, ba—." She replied, but he cut her off by lowering himself and putting his tongue on her body, lapping up the juices that had flown onto her.

He kissed and sucked along her midriff, sucking on her belly button as he looked up to her. The two delicious breasts were there, waiting for him, as he latched onto one and put his hand to work on the other.

Screams and moans of pleasure emanated from that hotel room that night, and they didn't stop until the morning.

The morning came with a whisper, the sun almost too afraid to show itself on the horizon as it hid behind the cloudy skies.

A heavy quilt of clouds smothered the morning, the grey an omen of exactly how Mercy felt that day. She had lived in the moment, in those exciting, exquisite moments of ecstasy—but now the time had come for her to come back to reality, and only have the moments she cherished live in her memories.

But then again, she was *exhausted*. Who wouldn't be after a night like that? Who wouldn't dream of having something like that happen to them over and over and over again, forever and ever, until their legs and spirit give out and it continues its sensual onslaught into the deepest, darkest crevices of their mind and thoughts.

Her knees ached at the thought of the magic that made her feel that ever so wonderful ache today. It was *everywhere*. Her neck, beautifully bruised with his marks of possession, felt the magic touch as she craned it sideways and back and forth. Her feet and hands made a little cracking sound as she stretched them, the feeling of quiet satisfaction washing over her as she did. And her face---it broke into the happiest smile for just a moment, almost falling into the trap of remembrance she was desperate to delay at least until she was back home.

Back home.

She had to get ready today and be in the air in just a few hours, and by God, her room was an absolute mess.

To be fair, Mercy wasn't exactly some neat freak. No, she cleaned after herself as anyone should, but she did not make a fuss about it either. This though, felt like someone had gone to town on her room.

'*Or rather, myself,*' she thought to herself and chuckled. Someone definitely did, and she could feel the sensations of pleasure in her head once again—just before she shook the thought away.

I have to get ready!

She scolded herself and her own filthy mind for never taking a break. The magic was still alive, but Mercy wanted to keep it that way. She did not want to face the gray skies of the world outside that room, outside from the golden drapes that bathed her room in blissful, tawny hues.

Articles of clothing were strewn about in her room, and the memories of the salacious, downright filthy activities that precluded the removal of those clothes came back to her as she picked each one.

The first was her shirt, white and ever-so-innocent, a display of her own purity—one would have thunk. But Mercy was anything but, and she remembered how he *tore* it off her, the few missing buttons from it evidence of the heat and passion he made her endure so long before taking that step.

Oh, *fuck me!* She whispered to herself, her hand snaking its way down her abdomen, down to that place she was aching in bliss, her own lips parting in the same way the other twins would be.

Mercy couldn't help but rub her palm over her underwear, letting herself feel the sensation once again.

Just a few strokes over the panties, and then I'm done. She thought.

But with every movement, every flicker of her fingers as they attempted to dig their way into her dampening crevice, the restrictions they found only heightened her senses, and what she felt at her own touch.

And in that feeling, Mercy couldn't keep her balance, and almost fell down to the floor, her hand caught between her legs as she regained her senses.

Her feet had shifted as she had lost her balance, and they landed on her bra. She remembered picking it out for the day, not particularly expecting her usual cotton comrades to have an audience, though this time, she was thankful that she wanted to feel good and had picked a lacy lingerie pair that *really* accented her very, very ample breasts with her petite frame.

She felt their soft fabric as she picked them up and was still quite amazed that they survived the throes of pleasure that had caused *him*, *Hiro*, to nearly tear them off before Mercy had to go back for a moment and take them off herself. And it took so deliciously long that he couldn't help but jump onto her breasts, not waiting to savor the feel, the shape, or even the tear-up-glass hardness of her nipples.

And there she was again, touching where he had touched, rubbing and flicking whichever way she could to remember every iota of the pleasure he made her feel as he launched his erotic attack.

I really need to pour some cold water on my face, she thought. She was absolutely losing it, and she had a plane to catch.

Quickly, she gathered up her trousers, her cardigan, and hurriedly shoved them inside her bag. There was no time to launder and fold anything just now. All that would have to wait because there was a burning fire inside her that was only waiting for its flames to be fanned a little bit more, and she couldn't risk tearing the only piece of clothing she was wearing for some bean flicking just yet. Mercy had a plane to catch.

It was something of a battle to keep her hands to herself for Mercy as she took a quick shower just after she packed. *I should win an award for this. Abnormal abstinence, it'll be called.*

But she couldn't help but admire herself in the mirror as she quickly did a once-over of the room, checking if anything else was left to pack.

No wonder why he was over me.

If there would ever be anyone worthy of being called half their age, it would have been her.

Mercy by name and merciless in her exquisite sexuality, she never was anyone to *not* flounder the wealth she had inherited—which, in this case, were legs that would go on forever and a waist so flat you could drum off of it.

She was a beauty, even in the years that her peers would be looking to get regular facelifts and liposuctions, beauty had been merciful on…well…Mercy.

The sun seemed to be far less shy now as Mercy left her hotel room and booked an Uber to the airport. It was a very slow Sunday, and she had to half-drag her things all the way out.

The drive, thankfully, was free of the erotic memories of the night before, free of the delicious little fuck-scapade, of the raunchy romp she had. She did, though, keep shifting and clutching her thighs together during the entire trip.

This was not going to be an easy flight. She thought as she made her way to the airport, and crossed the Departure section and went into Customs and Security. A female security guard gave her a once over, and every touch felt sensational as if reawakening the little nerves of ecstasy.

As soon as Mercy found her seat—by a window, too—she relaxed. There was enough legroom on this flight that Mercy had little to worry about when it came to constantly crossing her legs this way and that, trying her very best to contain that heat between her legs that just didn't go away.

But why would it?

She wanted that heat to stay there, to remain as a reminder of the treatment it had received, how his throbbing member had penetrated her deepest folds and revealed to herself places within her that she had yet to discover.

My Hiro. She remembered him as a man out of a dream, capeless, and even without any sort of a superhero uniform except for the lone visor of a naval officer to demonstrate his authority, his gloriously naked form being enough to adequately demonstrate everything else *just right.*

She didn't know who sat next to her right then. Maybe someone did. Maybe nobody did. Mercy was far too busy in her own thoughts, though thankfully with enough tact that she didn't shove her fingers down to her little love button right there. She had *that* much self-control, at least, very much contrary to what had transpired between her and Hiro.

Would she ever have that moment again? Would *they* ever have that moment again? With each other?

Maybe I can recreate that moment of meeting Hiro and then him 'meating' me!

Her imagination soon turned to *it*—that dreadnought between his legs that summoned wave after wave of pleasure within her, that swam proud in oceans as they made oceans of their own, each little whimper being the only thing she could muster as that anchor weight thrust into her little love tunnel.

"Fuck me!" came the command from her, from Mercy, as Hiro prepared himself behind her.

"Yes, Ma'am!" He exclaimed and grabbed the hips of a woman whose aching pussy was dripping with excitement and wet from the countless other times he had already deposited his load.

Mercy couldn't wait. She put her hands where they belonged and began her work on her stern, screaming in ecstasy as a single finger entered her, and Hiro's tongue joined in with it.

"Oh, Hiro, yes! Make me cum with your tongue!" She screamed, or rather, wailed, as her shaking legs felt her expertly handled tongue as it spoke in all vernaculars of sex and erotic pleasure.

But it was not enough. She had experienced ultimate pleasure, the one that no tongue or finger or foreplay in the world could ever hope to equal. She had experienced Hiro's superpower, that extra appendage that hung proudly just below his torso, and gave pleasures of a raw, carnal nature.

"Fuck, Hiro, I need your cock in me, *now*!" No woman could ever have said that last bit the way Mercy did, with quiet desperation, yet in a tone that made it clear—this naval officer could only ever obey.

Hands and legs on the bed, Mercy bent down like an animal begging to receive a good fucking, and Hiro obliged as he repositioned himself behind her, making sure she could have some extra grip if he needed.

Mercy couldn't help but flick and play with her own nipples as the excruciatingly long seconds passed, switching the hands she used as each one got tired of holding her up in position.

There was relief on her face when she felt his hand find its way to her nipples as well, helping her balance, and she could feel the *cock* flopping heavily against the back of her thighs. It was hot, quite literally, its heat being able to melt anything and everything it touched—and Mercy's legs certainly did melt when it did.

Hiro took his time with her, knowing how desperate she was, how immediate her needs were in that moment. He put the head just beside the entrance of her folders, and waited. He waited for Mercy to painfully wail and moan, to feel the agony of ecstasy and to feel the aching pain that brought so much pleasure to both of them.

His member was so hard it almost looked swollen from all the foreplay, the reddish being apparent against his otherwise tanned frame. He spent quite some time out at sea, and his pecs and chiseled chest glistened against the moonlight as his cock grazed her pussy, teasing an invite but never making an entrance.

"Please, Hiro." Mercy begged. "I need you."

"For what?" He asked, teasing her. He knew he could make her do whatever she wanted, and his cock would be the only gift that he would need to promise.

"Fuck. Me. Hiro." She turned half turned around as she answered, trying to sound commanding, but she failed this time.

Perfect. He thought. He needed her to beg, and he needed her to *need* it.

Yet he was still slow in his entrance, only letting his head enter her as his hands continued their exploration of her body. He touched her back, kissing it along the spine until he reached her neck, before he put his hands around her neck and gently thrust forward.

"Oh!" was all Mercy could muster, her mouth open and her kitty feeling itself part to accommodate the pulsating member.

"Aahhh, oooh."

Hiro kept it there, letting her feel the heat radiating from it, as Mercy gulped against his hands on her neck. The way Hiro took charge but was never too rough with her made her feel ever wetter than the cock buried in her, the latter being the reward, *his* reward, just as much as hers.

"Oh, baby, you feel so good…baby." Mercy had difficulty speaking in between breaths, her ample chest heaving as she rotated her hips, ass swaying as a result.

Slap!

Hiro gave her cheeks a good smack, and Mercy flinched, baring her teeth in a smile which only made her feel better, feel indescribable sensations in her pussy.

"You don't know the half of it, baby." Hiro replied as he slowly backed away, removing himself from her until only the head of his cock remained nestled there.

"You want it?" He was teasing again, and instead of waiting this time around, Mercy shifted backward, thrusting herself back and having him get back in deep where he belonged in her.

"Oh fuck!" This time, it was Hiro who said it, and Mercy smiled. She had him, and she was going to enjoy it.

There was no teasing anymore. Both of them knew that they were well past the play, and now, it was time to *fuck*.

The warmth of skin on skin filled the air as Hiro thrust back and forth, and Mercy could feel her tits bounce forward and backward with each thrust. She matched his movements, finding the rhythm as best she could, with her legs aching in pleasure and her mouth open as she moaned for release.

But he showed, yet again, the surprising resilience that Mercy had fallen in love with the short time she had known Hiro. Of course, they had already had a few rounds, so this was expected, but he remained rock solid throughout, growing harder and harder still as they both approached orgasm.

"Fuck, baby, you feel soo good inside me!" Her last bit turned into a squeal as he hit just the right spot, finding places within her she didn't know existed. Her folds were opening to welcome him and his thrusts, and as his member went back out until only the head remained in her, each movement hit her inner walls like fire. She could feel him pulsating, his swollen member begging just as she was many, many moments of pleasure ago.

And those moments of pleasure came, time and time again. Between thrusts, between touches, between little flicks of her nipple that Hiro did, or as his hands found their way to her front and rubbed her pussy; she came. Time and time again. Each orgasm was like a ripple across the ocean waves that didn't seem to end, each scream she made only welcoming Hiro to thrust harder.

Yet Mercy didn't feel like she needed a break. She needed more. Her pussy ached, but not at the post-orgasmic bliss—she needed him to cum, and she knew exactly how.

"Hey, hey, kiss me." She said as she positioned herself up, and Hiro's hand—almost on its own—found its way to her breast to keep her upright.

"Come here, babe." Hiro continued his thrusts inside her as she turned her head back, reached around to grab his head, and they locked their lips together.

Mercy could feel her own juices on his lips as their tongues danced together, lips clumsily touching in between his thrusts but finding their stride for a second or two.

"Mmmmhnn." She moaned in his mouth as they became one, hips and lips locked together, his thrusts slowing just a bit to accommodate their multifaceted lovemaking.

"Babe…" She started as she began to breathe after a kiss, but was cut off as Hiro's lips reached her in the next moment.

"Babe…are you…?" She laughed as his mouth was on hers once again, knowing full well that she would have to work to be able to do what she wanted.

"Close?" was all she could muster in between kisses, her breathing heavy, her breasts rising and falling with each little sip of the air that she could manage as she was getting railed by this hunk of a man.

"Hmm." Hiro's own response was one of urgency, his own face reddening at the prospect of a release. But this time, he felt like it would be a waste to lock himself inside her as he would find his own release, and as he looked at Mercy's face, he knew that it was what she wanted as well.

A few final thrusts followed, urgent and quick, and Mercy screamed and moaned his name.

"Oh, Hiro, oh fuck fucking fuck mee, aaah!" She screamed, and in the next moment, his member had left her, and Hiro turned her around like she weighed nothing, putting his face on hers.

They kissed but for a moment, as a more pressing one was fast approaching.

Hiro stood on his knees on the bed while Mercy got down on all fours, her face right in front of the swollen, pulsating love rod that he had used on her so many times and had been inside her moments ago.

It was pink at the head, thick and girthy like a veiny branch of a tree older than civilization itself. The shaft shared the tanned color of Hiro's skin, though it was a bit darker, and it shifted up and down on its own as Mercy felt its heat on her face.

She smiled as she looked up from her position at Hiro, and back again. His smooth, hairless pelvis was something she loved about him, and she gave him a kiss just below his abs as her hand softly grabbed the hardest piece of flesh she had ever touched in her life.

It was glorious, but like the many times she had already had it in her mouth, this was no time to savor the moment. She put her hand around it and jerked him off. Back and forth she went, grabbing the shaft and pulling it up as her lips reached its base and she licked it from base to head.

She put the head in her mouth like a lollipop and with a slurp, put her own saliva on it, unconsciously, as Mercy found herself drooling at the sight. It was already wet as a cock could be, and with her juices all over it, it didn't need any more lubing.

"I'm gonna cum, babe." Hiro said, voice low and growly, and Mercy assumed the position she needed to.

"Yes, sir!" She said, smiling, as she opened her mouth and prepared for what was to come.

She quickened her movements as she felt him getting closer, approaching that finish line, and Mercy closed her eyes.

And he erupted as he did, streaks of cum shooting from the tip of his cock like jets, finding their way into her mouth, on her face, her cheeks, her chin, and across her lips.

She quickly swallowed the first wave, and opened her eyes, and the cock was still pulsing, still aching for more to be released.

She quickly grabbed the base and opened her mouth, making sure as she took the member in, feeling each cum-stroke hit the back of her throat.

She sucked it all in as she released it from her mouth, and saw little droplets of cum begin to drip from the tip. She positioned it upward, and licked the cum from his cock well before it would fall on the bed and be wasted.

Hiro collapsed on the bed, looking proudly at the masterwork he had done in painting her with him, his batter covering her face like a perfect veil, and she smiled as little drops found their way into her lips from her cheeks and forehead. He saw her use her hands to scoop up anything and everything she could find, and with a slurp, take it all in.

He looked at the form in front of him, a woman in her prime, her hair tussled with a freshly-fucked look, something he had witnessed firsthand, though it looked far worse before they started this round.

He looked at her face, her plump, full lips as she licked them with her tongue. Her eyes were looking at his direction, but Mercy wasn't looking *at* him. She was somewhere else, in a world of her own, in total bliss.

He looked at her symmetrical face, her prominent jaw and the little shifting of the muscles on her neck as she sucked in his juices.

His eyes went downward, to her collarbone where some of his cum had found its way and in a sight so delicious, leaked down to the top of her breasts, which stood firm and contented. He looked at her nipples, brown and hard, surrounded by small areolas that perfectly accented the roundness of her tits, shaped just right for him to suckle on and hold on to.

His eyes trailed down, to her abdomen, her stomach, which showed a hint or two of ab muscles between the flat-yet-curvy surface.

Then, eyes following the direction he was going, he looked at the prize, the final destination, at a pussy where the clit was showing itself even now, jutting out like a cute little love button he could turn on with a flick of his finger, or a lap of the tongue.

The thighs that surrounded that pussy, though, were in a league of their own. Even sitting up as she was in the middle of the bed, her calf muscles accentuated themselves, and her thighs didn't lose their shapeliness. From the hip to her feet—and the rest of her, too—she was perfect. A woman through and through, and a woman who was made to be fucked. She was the muse to his member, slot to his key, and she was his for the night.

II – A Chance Encounter

Mercy was excited about coming to town. She had been anxious her entire flight, wondering if she'd be able to do everything she wanted in just a day or two before having to fly back home.

Starting out the day had been relatively simple. She had booked a hotel room for two days and nights and slept there as soon as her plane landed. She had arrived at night time, and as soon as she left her hotel room the next morning, it as like she was in a different world entirely.

Mercy was never good with directions or finding her own way around places. It always took her a good long while to recognize where she was going, and opting to go to a foreign country for the event was something she wasn't anticipating would be this confusing.

Still not particularly tech-savvy, she had accidentally changed the language of her phone to her current location. Some button she had tapped on in her haste to sleep that night, perhaps, and whatever happened then had given her a language she couldn't recognize at all. Even her phone would be useless here, and the only thing she knew was the address of her hotel and the airport.

It was a full-day, all-inclusive event. There would be little games, educational seminars, famous speakers, and whatnot. It was a place to network and enjoy yourself, the latter being the unofficial stance that almost every attendee took to heart.

But Mercy couldn't find the damn place, and even if she could have figured out a way to revert the language, her phone wasn't exactly bursting with energy. She had turned it off on her flight and after catching a ride to her hotel, neglected to put it on charge for the night. At just 1% battery, she'd be lucky to open up the maps app and put in a destination.

Her family was here too, and the plan was to have dinner after the event, but they didn't pick up the phone either. They weren't early risers, and while it was almost noon, Mercy didn't expect them to be up for a few hours at least.

The venue for the event should have been a short, ten-minute walk from the hotel she was staying at, but nothing looked even remotely similar to the photos in the pamphlets, perhaps all too outdated for it to be like that.

The crowd of people didn't help either. Each seemed all too busy, and none of them spoke any English. She could swear that she heard a few English words around her, and the people deliberately didn't help.

Perhaps it was fate that did that, too, as she'd soon discover. She would certainly have regretted it and would have gone home with exactly what she had expected—and nothing else—if some random stranger had given her all the right directions. They didn't, and looking back, Mercy was all too thankful for it.

Mercy stood among the crowd for about an hour, and each minute took some people with it, the crowd thinning as time passed. Soon, it was almost like only she remained at the sidewalk, and even the shops that should have been open at this hour of noon decided to shift away somewhere else, their cashiers and shopkeepers nowhere to be seen.

"Are you waiting for someone?" he asked her as she stood there all alone. Yes, *he* did.

She jumped as she looked behind him at the source of the voice, and *my*, what a source it was.

Standing tall, a hunky naval office clad in full uniform, standing at attention with his visor tucked in his right arm. Like in a suit of armor, of a knight, shining bright as the sun, white as the shining light, he appeared before her.

The long-sleeved, white shirt was smooth, pressed to perfection, and hugging oh-so-very-noticeable muscles that struggled to hide themselves beneath the sleeves. Lines of gold were etched on the shoulders, like pauldrons of a knight, gleaming in the sun as they anchored the white fabric of his dress shirt.

His trousers were sharp, white and flared at the bottom, accented perfectly with the black leather shoes that completed the look.

But the man donning that uniform was a sight to behold on his own. He sported a jaw so perfectly shaped one would think the gods themselves made it happen, and his eyes, even in the sun, were unmistakably dark and striking, framed perfectly with short hair and a clean-shaven face.

Mercy was startled; she could barely speak. There he stood, in his uniform, this very handsome naval officer with the most beautiful, dark eyes she had ever seen. He had the most intense stare.

"Yes!" she finally stated after a gulp or two. Whatever this beast of a man was, in a single moment and with a few words, had awoken a fire inside her.

Mercy was a widow, a woman who had lost her husband not too long ago, but in her life, there had been little in the ways of sex even before the accident that took her husband's life. She had married her high-school sweetheart, and like many of those relationships go, the fire that had kept them stuck to each other had died down after the decades had passed.

But she was never one to just give herself up in those situations. She had always cared for herself, for her looks, and made sure that she never really let herself go off the deep end, especially after her husband stopped paying attention to her.

Instead, she paid attention to herself, working out almost daily, finding her own happiness in her own company rather than seeking out anyone to start anew—or even for a single night. At the moment, she was not thinking of a man or any relationship of any kind, yet this man didn't spark the fire of a relationship within her. There was something primal in how she felt, a heat, a wetness that came in an instant, and Mercy was at his mercy.

She imagined herself, putting her hands on his chest as he wore nothing but his visor, his nakedness bathed in the golden sun and the beach where she stood, even in her imagination withing she had been wearing a bikini so she could just pull on a string or two and slide the two articles of clothing that remained, matching her naked form with his.

She imagined kissing him, the sunrays shining in between their lips as they slowly locked them together, and her legs finding their way around him, snaking across his hips so she could thrust her hips forward and back, feeling his growing hardness against her.

Mercy wondered just how big, just how thick he would be. It certainly felt like a shaft, a rod, a pipe, or perhaps the thickest, veiny, most deliciously hard cock she had ever had the pleasure of laying her eyes on. Her husband had been the only man she ever knew that way, and her little escape into the world of smut and salacious little stories was the only cocksure companion she ever had.

Even naked, she grinded against him, his cock dangerously close to entering her, and a little whimper escaping her lips every time she felt its touch on her entrance, and his touch, all over her as his tongue invaded her mouth.

Mercy was infatuated with this officer and she couldn't remember the last time someone made her feel this way. Catching herself, she realized that she had been standing there staring at him, and the man knew exactly the effect that he was having on her.

"Oh, ahem. I…uhh…" She began, stammering her way through her words as she shifted her balance on each leg, standing awkwardly on the sidewalk.

"Ma'am, breathe. Take your time." His voice was deep, clear, and direct. Mercy clasped her legs together, trying as best she could to stifle the heat between her legs without putting her hands there right in front of the man.

"Yeah, I, uhh, got lost. I'm waiting for my family, you see…" She began, but he held up an authoritative hand and interjected.

"Hang on a second, I'll be right back," he stated and briskly walked in the other direction.

As she watched him, she couldn't help but admire the way he walked, as well as that delicious rump that he sported, perfectly shapely and athletic, even from a distance and with pressed, ironed trousers covering it. There was just something about a man in uniform. An authority that made her feel like putty like she would obey his command even if he commanded her to strip and suck like his personal fuck toy.

And arousal was just one of the million things Mercy felt in that moment as her head ran wild and imagination took over, filthy and unfiltered in how she obeyed his commands.

A look was all he needed to make her go down to her knees and begin. Even flaccid, it stood like a dangling carrot atop her, threatening to break anything it invaded, and Mercy wanted nothing more than *it* to break *her*.

Obediently, she stroked it back and forth, lightly, sensually, as she felt it getting harder and harder at her touch. Her lips quickly found their way all over and around the heated rod, coating it with her spit, her saliva, and feeling it engulf her mouth as she took it in.

She gagged and gaggled as she sucked, taking it in and shoving it as deep as she could in her mouth. She wasn't some expert cocksucker who knew exactly what technique to get him going, but whatever she did—and whatever he was—the both of them had their eyes in the back of their head in pleasure.

She felt her pussy ache, the nub getting wet as her hand found its way there, palming her entrance as she licked and sucked and suckled on his cock. To say she was around would be an understatement. For so long she had worked on herself, not really thinking just how good she looked beneath her clothes, especially so for her age. Even women in their 20s would kill for the proportions she had, and this man—she was willing to give it all to him, to be at his mercy.

She thought about what she wanted him to do and how she wanted him to do it to her. She became wet with lust just thinking about him, and she didn't even know where he had gone.

He came over from behind her and tore her clothes up as she got down on all fours. With no fanfare or celebration, he was inside her in an instant, finding no resistance as her already very wet folders parted to see his achingly large member through.

Right there, on the sidewalk next to the beach, she would scream his name. The name she hadn't even asked of, and the name that would be on her lips endlessly, screamed out into the world with each thrust he made.

He would grab her hands and use them to thrust forward with force, and she would only match the rhythm of his movements, her hips and his matching their style like the synchronicity of a dance number.

"Are you cumming?" He asked in between his thrusts, and she could hardly answer. She was out of breath, and he never stopped fucking her as she struggled to elicit any sound other than her moans.

"Cum, babe. I'm cumming too." His voice whispered in her ear as she felt his pulsating member explode inside her, filling every nook and cranny with his fluids.

"Are you coming, Ma'am?"

And at that moment, she quickly regained her senses. He was standing nearby at a shop, and holding out a cell phone for her. It was a cellphone, and Mercy cleared her throat as she smiled at him, hoping he hadn't figured out what was going on in her mind, and just how wet she was between her thighs.

He made a couple of calls for her and let her know where she needed to be. Mercy couldn't remember what he said to her, at least, not anymore as she was back on her seat in the plane, heading home.

Whatever he said, though, didn't matter. It was only his voice that she focused on and the third leg that a voice like that would have.

At that moment she wanted to be on top of him, riding his pole, feeling the sweat drip down on his chest as it made it glisten even more in the sun. As he was giving her the directions, she was looking at his uniform for his name and she wanted to make sure there was no wedding band. She wanted him for herself. This wasn't just a guy she was standing next to. This was a *man*. A real man. Hunkier than the hunkiest, and she wanted nothing more than him to treat her with a fuck—or a thousand—she wouldn't ever forget.

Hiro.

That's what the nametag said, and that is what she did, too.

"Thank you, Mr…" She glanced once more at the tag as she said it, making sure she wasn't mistaken. "…Hiro." A knowing smile formed across her face. She couldn't help it, and her eyes squinted in sexual desire.

Mercy swayed her hips as she walked away from the office, accenting her ass for him as she felt his eyes on her—or rather—or ample backside.

She wanted nothing more than to look back as she was walking away, but decided against it. She knew she would only long for him more if she did, and she was already a nervous wreck in front of this man. She was a grown-up woman, acting like a child who had just found a new favorite toy. She couldn't help but smile, wondering if she would ever see him again. She didn't want this to be the last time, and if ever would be looking back at her, at her hips and ass swaying about, and if he would have the look of lust that she hoped he would, it would be tragically unfortunate, because she would pounce on him right then.

This was a man who had awakened every desire and passion inside of her. He had lit the fire of ecstasy with nothing but a look, a few words, and just…being him. There was nothing sexual about the things he did, but because *he* did them, they oozed sex just as much as Mercy's own pussy oozed her own fluids.

She wanted to feel him, his cock, inside of her mouth and pussy. She wanted him to erupt inside her, to mark her with his flesh, and make her his own little plaything to fuck as he pleased.

But as she walked, she didn't look back. She needed to cool down anyway, because she'd be entering a very public domain soon, and she didn't want to look like a flustered woman begging for the man to fuck her.

The event was…as expected. The initial excitement had been entirely overshadowed by someone else, and *something* else. Half the time she imagined herself on stage, displaying her sometimes amateurish and sometimes expert-level skill at making him cum with her hands, mouth, lips, pussy, thighs, and even feet. The crowd cheered her on as she demonstrated different positions, and Hiro obliged and handled her directions expertly as well.

Their minds were almost as if linked together, and whoever spoke at the seminar had their voice drowned out by the sound of skin on sweaty skin ramming together, and the moans that escaped their lips.

It was a tough afternoon to get through, and when evening rolled around, she made it to where her family were, a rather humble yet spacious abode where the dinner table was already set when she made it there.

She exchanged pleasantries, had a cold shower before and after dinner to cool off, and wondered what else the night could have brought. She had enjoyed her time here, dinner with her family, the event too—but only one thing preoccupied her thoughts, and she couldn't escape them.

She could not stop thinking of him as she walked back to her hotel room, thinking, 'What if.'

I wonder what he could be doing now, she wondered to herself. If only he were there in her bed.

She felt the satin, velvety sheets of the hotel room on her bare skin. It was just after evening, but she was already ready for bed, though she didn't want to be.

She wanted someone else there, and she knew exactly who.

She wanted him. His cock. His body. His smell and weight on her.

She decided that she would go out that night. She couldn't stop thinking of him and she wanted to find him. Tonight, Mercy would be on the prowl.

She put on the attire she was wearing before. A shirt, pants, and a cardigan. She put on her lacy bra and panties, a lingerie set she had mistakenly packed but had secretly wanted to wear at the event.

It was, once again, a short walk to the area where she had first seen the officer. She expected him to be difficult to find, though she thought she'd have to ask around. It wasn't as if people wouldn't have noticed a large, tall, handsome naval officer in full uniform walking across the boardwalk.

To her surprise, he was right there where she had left him hours ago, talking to a shopkeeper.

They made eye contact, and he immediately recognized her. His visor was on the shop's counter, and as they locked eyes, he stood up straight, put on his visor, and walked briskly over to her.

"Lost again, ma'am?" he asked. "I could give you a map, but if you'd prefer, I'll be happy to assist you." He sounded just as confident as last time, but his tone was slightly…different. There was a familiarity in his voice, mixed in with a hunger that wouldn't have been obvious if not for his wry smile.

"I'm not lost, sir." She said, eyes locked on him, her hands on her hips. "I'm in the right place." she breathed out the words, and his eyebrows raised in response.

"Please, call me Hiro." He said, straightening his shirt. "And what are you looking for in this fine beachside this evening?"

"Satisfaction."

"Oh, really?" He chuckled, knowing what would transpire next, but Mercy saw that he was getting in his groove, thinking that he would smooth his way into her. But she had other plans.

"I'll be leaving tomorrow, and there is no time for pleasantries." Mercy held up her hand the same way he had that morning. "My hotel room, now."

III - Reunion

"Hiro, I want you and I want you to come with me." She said, hands on her hips still. She watched his face closely as his smile grew wider at the fact that this hot older woman was ready to pounce on him, a cougar that had found her prey. "I hope you can get away for a minute."

He smiled, "Baby, I got all the time in the world." He laughed, and Mercy followed suit. He was behaving exactly as she wanted him to, as she would have wanted him to. Prim and proper like Prince Charming, glowing in the sun, and now in the cloudy night, as a knight in shining armor. And smooth as a player but humble and well put together, too.

The route back to the hotel was short, hardly ten minutes, but Mercy couldn't wait that long. She wanted him now, and if she would get an Uber, they'd have to take the long way, and it would be a ten-minute ride to the other side of the boardwalk where she was staying.

She called an Uber and explained to him where she needed to go. She didn't look at him but knew that the driver understood his assignment and, at cruise speed, went on his way to the hotel.

"So where are we going?" Hiro asked as they started with the drive. "We are going back to my hotel. I want you and I know you want me too", she said seductively, her hands touching his and grabbing them as she placed them on her thighs. Hiro silently let her do whatever she wanted and didn't question or inquire further.

Mercy put her hand in Hiro's pants and felt his hard flesh. He felt so damn good. It had been a long time since she had a hard cock in her hands, a *real* cock, not something out of her imagination. He closed his eyes and silently, with his mouth closed, moaned as she began to play with his cock from outside of his trousers.

Her hands snaked their way into his trousers, pushing aside his underwear as she found his hardness, grabbing it in her hands. She stroked it back and forth and up and down as his hands went upward to touch her breasts, feeling their smoothness from over the fabric.

The little cab was dark, and the lights in the streets weren't exactly illuminating the interior of the car, and Mercy was thankful for that. A single button of hers went loose as Hiro found his way to her bra, stimulating her nipples from over the lacy fabric as she moaned.

To shut her up—or rather, to shut the both of them up—they started passionately kissing. As he put his hand between her legs and felt the wetness of her pussy, she jumped, laughing into his mouth as his tongue spoke musical words to her.

At that moment, they had arrived back at the hotel. Once the Uber driver was paid, Hiro and Mercy walked into the hotel, towards the elevator, in a dazzling display of self-control, at least out in the open, as they sought to at least reach the hotel room before attacking each other with hunger and lust.

But once inside, past the lobby, they could not keep their hands off of one another. The wait for the elevator didn't happen, as Mercy pressed the button and Hiro pushed her against the wall next to it. They got busy kissing, touching, feeling, grinding, gyrating.

The ding was both welcome and a sound that Mercy didn't want to hear. The feeling of being worshipped the way she was; she didn't want that feeling to end, but of course, even she knew that she couldn't just push him to the floor and ride him right there— regardless of how much her fantasies made that possible.

Inside the elevator, they continued to kiss, touch, and tease. Mercy and Hiro barely made it into the room, both stripping off each other's clothing.

The cardigan came off in a flutter, and Mercy could feel the air, hot and heavy, on her arms and her short-sleeved shirt. But soon, Hiro's hands were on her and with a deft swing, tore off the white cloth from their buttons.

Things were quiet for a moment, as Hiro's face turned into one of gilt, like a deer caught in the headlights. He waited for Mercy's reaction, and she began giggling, laughing, and so did Hiro.

"I thought you didn't have replacements for a moment there." He breathed sighs of relief, and she pushed him by the chest, his own shirt half unbuttoned, feeling the hardness. She grabbed his shirt by both sides and attempted—her very best of attempts—to tear off his shirt, too.

"Expensive, love. And it's a uniform, treat it with care." He whispered, giggling as they unbuttoned the rest together, and he tossed it aside. "Care, I said, not respect." Hiro laughed, displaying his white undershirt stretching beneath the unmistakable ab muscles and huge pecs he sported.

Their pants were the next to go. His belt came off with a swing, and in seconds, he was just in his underwear. Mercy began to take off her own pants, too, but Hiro stopped her. Neither said anything, but the man simply took it slow, revealing bit by bit of the woman, savoring the experience of unwrapping a gift he wanted to play with all night long.

After the pants were off, both of them looked at each other, parting slightly to take a good look at what stood before them.

Mercy's hand reached up to her lips and she bit her finger slightly, eyes screaming *'fuck me'* while the rest of her body breathed heavily at the thought. The lacy bra and panties hugged her just right, not too loose and not too tight. She was especially proud at the way her bra made her breasts feel, as if a pair of soft yet brawny hands were supporting them—through those magnificent tits of hers needed no supporting.

She looked over at Hiro, six packs of chiseled, raw muscle, each hard curve defined and shapely, his thighs and glutes standing at rapt attention as they attempted very successfully to support the hulking beast that was situated right in between them.

Looking at his hard member, then his eyes, Mercy reached behind her back and unsnapped the bra she was wearing, freeing her breasts from their rather comfortable confines and into the heavy air of the hotel room, and Hiro's gaze followed her every movement.

They were perfect. Shapely round globes of pure pleasure, heavy as if waiting to be sucked and suckled on, but definitely not the kind a 40-something woman would have. They were supple and invited him to be touched and felt, their succor hidden beneath the tiny brown areolas and the hard nipples that tipped them.

And Hiro did just that. Approaching Mercy, he first grabbed her by her head and her waist and pulled her in for a kiss. They exchanged their fluids, and their tongues danced together as Hiro shifted his position downward, his lips and mouth reaching her neck.

He suckled. He bit her neck lightly, and she laughed and screamed in delight, pleasure forming like pulsing waves all over her body and skin.

Then, his lips tilted, and so did his head, and he came to the place he wanted to be. He kissed around her breasts, in the middle, between her chest, under them, and around the nipples. He teased her as she grabbed his head, lightly guiding him to the central treasure troves.

Once his mouth found its way onto her right nipple, she took a breath in and released moans of pleasure.

"Ohhhhh. Oooo." She cooed, stroking his hair and biting her lip as he drank her in. She wasn't lactating, but she could swear she felt some milk trickle from her and into his mouth.

He shifted to the left nipple, replacing his mouth on the right one with a soft yet firm hand, and gave it an equal treatment.

But the ultimate prize was waiting, still covered, which was the case for both of them. His mouth trailed downward, across her midriff that she kept toned and fit, and reached her panties, black and sexy as herself.

"I want to taste you." He said as he took her underwear from her thighs in between his teeth and slowly pulled himself downward, taking the lacy fabric with him. Slowly, Mercy lifted one foot after the other, allowing Hiro to remove her panties from her, and he bit on them as they finally released from her grasp. He smiled and growled like an animal, and Mercy breathed heavily, silent, with moans the closest things to words she could manage to muster then.

But he didn't bury his face in between her legs just yet. Hiro got up and carried her to the bed, and Mercy felt her feet graze his rock-hard cock, still hidden beneath his underwear, as he picked her up.

He dropped her on the bed with a thud, and she bounced once or twice before landing on it, and Mercy shifted her position back. She crawled to the foot of the bed, and she sensually opened up her legs to show him what he desired.

Her pussy lips were on fire, opened up to his gaze like a lily to the heat. He knelt before the foot of the bed, Mercy gazing down at him hungrily, and he stared at her hungrily back.

Eyes locked on each other, he began with her feet, licking them, sucking on her toes and kissing up her calf. Reaching the thighs, his eyes were on her, and she felt almost ticklish as Hiro kissed and bit her thighs. She ached to feel his mouth on her right then.

"Come on, baby, fuck me with your mouth." She stated, but it felt more like a question in the way she made it sound, almost like she didn't know what he was going to do next, and she was excited in anticipation.

"I will fuck you with more than just my mouth, babe," Hiro replied, a mischievous smile on his lips, and he dove down to munch on her muffin like nobody else ever had before.

She screamed and moaned in ecstasy as he began to lick her pussy, delight across her face and in her voice with each lap of his tongue. She caressed his head as she yearned for more, her pussy becoming wetter and wetter as Hiro lapped up the juices that overflowed from her, the smell of her fluids intoxicating for the both of them. His cock threatened to break free from his underwear, and it, too, had gotten so hard that it almost hurt. Hiro decided he would speed up the process, just a tiny little bit, adding a few more stimulants to really drive up the pleasure.

He stopped to breathe for a moment and brought his hand to her face, two of his fingers pressing forward to her lips as she instinctively opened them, allowing his fingers inside as she licked them and made them wet with her saliva.

She knew what was coming, and it was *her.*

Her mouth opened, but she couldn't even bring out any sound as his fingers entered her. One, then two, and she felt herself tighten around them as his mouth worked on her pussy, his other hand around her thigh, keeping her in place. One of her hands caressed his hair and head, and the other kneaded at her breast.

On occasion, his hands came over hers, too, and she got some extra attention on her tits. Every now and then, for a second or two, he would stop, keep his hand between her legs and finger her as he'd get up to kiss her or suck on her tits. It was a brilliant switch of sensations as he changed up where she felt all the pleasures she could.

And she was getting close, closer and closer to the precipice as he alternated, and then the door opened.

She came, time and time again, waves upon waves and oceans upon oceans of girl-cum feeling like they were escaping her, erupting from her. Mercy had never really squirted ever before, not with her husband and not on her own. This was something else, a sensation that left her legs shaking and her body convulsing almost on its own.

Breathing, heavily, Mercy was completely out of it, out of her breath, out of this world, in a world of her own at that moment. Eyes closed, she was smiling as she let the post-orgasmic bliss wash over her, feeling the satisfaction of finishing like *that* engulf her mind, body, and soul all over.

Hiro grabbed her and picked her up from the bed, but only to drag her just a little bit in the middle of it. He climbed on the bed, sitting up as he positioned her the way he wanted, and Mercy was all smiles, too when she came to and realized what was happening.

Hiro looked into her eyes as he positioned himself just at her entrance, and even in her entranced state, Mercy snaked her hand below, reaching down to his cock and guiding it to her fuck hole.

But Hiro resisted and waited.

"Wait, baby. Tell me you are alright, first. Tell me you want this."

It took a moment for Mercy to realize what he was asking her, and what his intentions were in doing so. It endeared her to him, and she shed a single tear of happiness.

He was asking for consent, even now, completely naked and atop her.

"Of course, baby. Fuck me to kingdom come. Fuck me till my legs give out and I cannot walk anymore. Show no mercy."

And with that, he thrust, a single stroke that made her senses go haywire, her brain a jumbled mush of sensual sensations and erotic pleasure.

A few strokes and she was already cumming and convulsing, a display of womanly satisfaction that Mercy had rarely ever felt before.

He picked her up and pushed her against the wall, sliding his fingers in her wet pussy as he prepared to enter her once again.

"Beautiful," he murmured as he drank in the exquisite, sexual creature before him. Hiro couldn't help but admire her time and time again, wondering what he did in life to desire this complete woman, this buxom, beautiful, bodacious minx, to be welcoming him inside her with total and reckless abandon, screaming words of filth and ecstasy combined.

The more he probed her pussy, the wetter she became, coating his cock in love juices and only heightening the pleasure she felt. He began to play with her clit, and Mercy moved her hips back and forth with him.

"You like it? Squirt for me!" He whispered in his ear as he fucked her.

And she did. Mercy moaned and began to shake uncontrollably. "I'm losing control, please don't stop!" she exclaimed. Hiro gently grabbed her chin and stuck his tongue in her mouth. "Surrender to me," he stated, a command more so than a request, words not just said in the heat of the moment, but with purpose and clarity of sexual action.

She placed her legs up on his shoulder and he began to fuck her just the way she wanted him to. The back of her knees were on his shoulders, and her feet were perched up in the air, flailing around as he used her pussy.

He thrust her in the air and began to lick her pussy once more. Mercy enjoyed every moment of it. He turned her around, spread her ass and thrust his hard cock inside her pussy. She placed her hands against the wall and bounced up and down on his cock. "Fuck me harder"! She screamed.

"You like this cock, baby"? He asked. It was a rhetorical question, but Mercy was all too happy to answer with enthusiasm.

"Ah yeah, you feel so fucking good! "

"Work that ass for me, bounce on this cock!" He grabbed her neck and kissed her, the erotic asphyxiation making her little climaxes even better.

He was perfect. Perfect in shape and for her, perfectly painful in his size, and perfectly fierce in his lovemaking—or perhaps, love-fucking—as he mercilessly spread her apart every which way.

And he had quite the stamina, too, never losing his rhythm or slowing down unless he wanted to. He was in total control and Mercy loved it, a hunk of a man and a hunk of a lover, sensationally accomplished in his sexual endurance.

She threw her head back and matched his rhythm, moaning for more. He picked her up and laid her on the bed. She wrapped her legs around his neck as he thrust his cock inside her wet folds, caressing her and sucking on her breasts.

He explored every inch of her body, kissing every piece of it he could lay his eyes, hands, or lips upon, and all the while Mercy only begged for more.

They did not want the night to end. "I want you to ride me, baby. Ride my cock, please, babe." He spoke with sexual urgency. He had kept his cool for so long, and he was beginning to struggle.

Mercy climbed on top and began to ride him. "Just like that, baby. Oh yeah, just like that." As she was riding his cock, he thrust back against her and spanked her ass, and she screamed with passion and pain in equal measure. She continued to ride his cock as he spanked her. "Oh baby, you're going to make me cum"! she exclaimed.

"I want to make you cum, cum for me, baby!" He spoke with gritted teeth and a breathless voice.

Mercy screamed in ecstasy as she began to climax. She couldn't remember the last time she felt so good, though she would have if she had her senses in that moment, because he had made her feel just that good moments ago.

Right now, though, she wanted him to cum too.

"Are you close?" She asked.

"I'm fucking cumming!" He threw his head back.

Mercy lifted her legs on the bed and locked them around his hips as he continued to thrust, filling her up as he shot his load inside her.

He fell beside her, breathless, and Mercy lay there, too, happily filled, his cum leaking from her pussy. She was in total bliss, completely taken by the sensation, as they both tried to catch their breaths, trying their best to look into each other's eyes but unable to keep up.

*****

The night welcomed much more than that moment, because neither Hiro nor Mercy were done. Of course, Hiro didn't know, but Mercy was not going to be able to stay, even for another day. She had absolutely no choice but to make the most of this night and make the most she did.

After their debaucherously delicious romp, they both decided to take a shower, but in their ecstatic states, they both knew and didn't really take into account that they would come out of the bathroom filthier than they had entered it.

This time, Mercy didn't want him to cum inside her—not because she didn't want it, but because she wouldn't have time for anything else. She told him to shower her with his love, his baby batter, his fuck fluids, and shower her he did.

She swallowed every drop, licking his cock clean, then trying to pump out more from him for good measure.

He, too, pinned her against the shower wall and buried his face in between her legs, pulling one leg over his shoulder while her other balanced on the floor. Mercy put her hand on his head, too, because if she hadn't, she'd be falling on the floor.

Even in the shower, water falling on their bodies, they were hot and sweaty from all the fucking they couldn't stop doing. Somehow, even after cumming twice in quick succession, Hiro was able to get hard again, and this time, Mercy took her time, playing with his cock, dancing on him, having him lift her up and bounce on his member as he had her in the middle of the shower.

Her large breasts bounced up and down, and Hiro tried to catch them with his mouth. Laughing, Mercy took them in her hands and guided her nipples to his lips, and he happily cooed like a baby as he suckled, the areolas already chapped with the amount of tit-sucking he had done that evening.

His fingers, too, received no mercy. Wet from her juices, the skin wrinkled—almost ribbed—it only increased the pleasure, Mercy felt when he slid them inside her, thrusting as she climaxed again and again.

Coming out of there was a challenge of its own. Mercy didn't know exactly when she or Hiro fell asleep, but they probably didn't exactly decide to because the next morning, when she woke up, they were all over the bed.

His head was on the foot of the bed, laying down upside-down, and she was only halfway on it, her arms resting more on the floor than the side of the bed, too. Mercy figured that they had collapsed making love, a fitting end to a night where satisfaction was the only requirement, because what else could two people like them hope for other than to be fucked so good they couldn't even function properly enough to sleep right.

IV - Farewell

The next morning was still a bit overcast, yet it had that fresh feeling of the post-rain effect, and Mercy could smell the rain from her hotel room, too. They had opened the windows a bit to allow the smell to escape in the night, otherwise nobody needed evidence of their fuck-scapade that night to tell what had transpired in the room. The smell alone was of pure sex, and anybody entering could have put two and two together from nearing the room through the hallways alone.

Hiro, though, was an early riser, and despite the very immediate and very appealing shaft that rose alongside him in the morning, Mercy was in no state to even just lay there and let him do his thing. Her memories of last night were still *too good* to just have him go 'wham bam thank you, ma'am' on her—and he probably would not have wanted it either.

Despite the events of the night, he was a gentleman, and perhaps more so *because* of what happened last night. He was always so welcoming, so sexy, and so attentive to her needs.

Being a man of the uniform, though, he couldn't stay, and as Mercy woke up at the sound of him taking a shower, even half-asleep, she couldn't help but lick her lips as he emerged from the shower, gloriously naked in form.

Her flight was that day, at noon, and there were still plenty of hours to go, but they couldn't possibly spend any more time together. The night had been magical and magically spontaneous, and it was time to go now.

Being the gentleman that he was, he woke her up some time later, a breakfast tray in his hands as he lay next to her in bed, showered and ready. His collar buttons were undone, and he was wearing his undershirt with his uniform still unbuttoned. It gave a really sexy look to him that Mercy couldn't help but stare at as he took a bite of a sandwich and a sip of coffee.

"How long are you going to be here?" he asked.

"I fly back home today," she replied, wiping the sleep from her.

"Damn, I wish you would stay longer. I would have liked to take you out to dinner and spend more time with you. I really enjoyed our night together." He said, reaching over to her face and brushing off a few strands of hair from her face to the side.

Mercy had enjoyed their night together as well, but she knew she had to return home soon, and he had to return to the naval station. Duty called, and Mercy knew that even if fate would never let them cross paths again, last night was something to remember forever, in cherished memories and the wettest of dreams that she knew she'd be having the rest of her life, his achingly beautiful cock never leaving her imagination.

As much as she wanted to stay with him, she knew it was impossible. Hiro placed his hand on hers and caressed her gently. "May I have your number?" he asked. "I would really like to stay in touch with you, I'd love to see you again…if…that's okay with you…?"

Mercy chuckled. His confidence, and the lack of it at times, was cute—endearing almost. Here he was, next to the woman whom he'd shown the time of her life, and he was being nervous at asking for her number. True, he had put her in a position where it would be difficult for her to refuse, but not in a million years would she refuse *anything* he wanted from her, or for her to do, or for him to do to her, or vice versa, and the million other combinations that could go with all that.

"I'd like that too. Next time, our love session will be much longer!" Mercy laughed, and Hiro joined in with her.

At that moment, they both stood up and Hiro embraced Mercy. He held her in his arms and they kissed gently, but passionately, like two lovers parting for the day but still not wanting to let each other go.

"Thank you for your service, sir!" she said happily. The Uber had just come, and they were standing outside the hotel, embracing.

Hiro smiled and said, "I'm happy you enjoyed my service. Next time, I will dock in your port for much longer, and you'll enjoy all the pleasures of a full shore leave!"

"I'm sure, for now, though, I'm satisfied," she said, before kissing him and grabbing his crotch. "*Very* satisfied."

They hugged and kissed once more and she watched as his Uber drove away.

Mercy shifted in her seat on the plane, smiling to herself, thinking of that amazing, passionate night they had, and the possibilities that the future held. Oh yeah, she *definitely* would stay in touch with him. Relaxed and satisfied, she would keep this feeling and this memory to herself for as long as she possibly could.

Mercy was excited for the future because she knew they would see each other again. And when they would, she would recount each moment of their tale, of red desire and passionate jaunts, convulsing in orgasm at each retelling.

www.ingramcontent.com/pod-product-compliance
Lightning Source LLC
Chambersburg PA
CBHW040845010826
48978CB00012BB/900